C00 756 447X

KU-730-673

This Faber
book belongs to:

..........................................

# Praise for Macavity

'I love MaCATity.' (Me – It's Macavity.)
'Yes that's what I said, MaCATity, because he looks like my cat and he is a very very funny naughty naughty cheat. And my name is on the cover (Arthur Robins).'

Robin, age 4, and mum, Donna

'This was fun to read to my little sister. I read the story and she shouted "Macavity's not there!" a lot and in her loudest voice.'

Hal, age 11

'We loved this book! We read it once, then Hazel asked me again the next day to read the story about the cat "they can't find".'

Hazel, age 4, and mum, Shona

'I like the funny police dog and the naughty cat!' Otto, age 6

'All the cats are naughty, aren't they – but Macavity is the naughtiest.'

Seb, age 4

| LEISURE AND CULTURE DUNDEE | |
|---|---|
| C00756447X | |
| Bertrams | 05/11/2015 |
| | £6.99 |
| FIN | |

For Chris and Kate
A. R.

From the original collection, 'respectfully dedicated to those friends who have assisted its composition by their encouragement, criticism and suggestions: and in particular to Mr. T. E. Faber, Miss Alison Tandy, Miss Susan Wolcott, Miss Susanna Morley, and the Man in White Spats. O. P.'

First published in 1939 in *Old Possum's Book of Practical Cats*
by Faber and Faber Ltd,
Bloomsbury House, 74—77 Great Russell Street, London WC1B 3DA
This edition first published in 2015

Printed in China

Illustrations © Arthur Robins, 2015

Design by Ness Wood

A CIP record for this book is available from the British Library

HB ISBN 978—0—571—32482—8
PB ISBN 978—0—571—32483—5

10 9 8 7 6 5 4 3 2 1

All rights reserved

© T. S. Eliot, 1939, Copyright renewed © 1967 Esme Valerie Eliot

FSC
www.fsc.org
MIX
Paper from responsible sources
FSC® C017606

→ A FABER PICTURE BOOK ←

# Skimbleshanks

Written by T. S. Eliot

Illustrated by
Arthur Robins

ff

FABER & FABER

There's a whisper down the line at 11.39
When the Night Mail's ready to depart,
Saying 'Skimble where is Skimble
has he gone to hunt the thimble?

'We must find him or the train can't start.'

All the guards and all the porters and the
stationmaster's daughters
They are searching high and low,

Saying 'Skimble where is Skimble
for unless he's very nimble
Then the Night Mail just can't go.'

At 11.42 then the signal's nearly due
And the passengers are frantic to a man—
Then Skimble will appear and he'll
    saunter to the rear:
He's been busy in the luggage van!

You may say that by and large it is Skimble
    who's in charge
Of the Sleeping Car Express.
From the driver and the guards to the
    bagmen playing cards
He will supervise them all, more or less.

Down the corridor he paces and examines all
    the faces
Of the travellers in the First and in the Third;

He establishes control by a regular patrol
And he'd know at once if anything occurred.

He will watch you without winking and he
sees what you are thinking
And it's certain that he doesn't approve

Of hilarity and riot, so the folk are
    very quiet
When Skimble is about and on the move.

You can play no pranks with Skimbleshanks!
He's a Cat that cannot be ignored;

Oh it's very pleasant when you have found
   your little den
With your name written up on the door.

And the berth is very neat with a newly
   folded sheet
And there's not a speck of dust on the floor.

There is every sort of light—you can make it dark or bright;

There's a button that you turn to make a breeze.

There's a funny little basin you're supposed to wash your face in

And a crank to shut the window if you sneeze.

Then the guard looks in politely and will ask
   you very brightly
'Do you like your morning tea weak or strong?'

But Skimble's just behind him and was ready
  to remind him,
For Skimble won't let anything go wrong.

And when you creep into your cosy berth
And pull up the counterpane,

You are bound to admit that it's very nice
To know that you won't be bothered by mice—

You can leave all that
to the Railway Cat,

The Cat of the Railway Train!

In the middle of the night he is always
    fresh and bright;
Every now and then he has a cup of tea

With perhaps a drop of Scotch while he's keeping on the watch,

Only stopping here and there to catch a flea.

You were fast asleep at Crewe and so you never knew
That he was walking up and down the station;

You were sleeping all the while he was busy
    at Carlisle,
Where he greets the stationmaster with
    elation.

But you saw him at Dumfries, where he summons the police
If there's anything they ought to know about:

When you get to Gallowgate there you do not have to wait—
For Skimbleshanks will help you to get out!

He gives you a wave of his long brown tail
Which says: 'I'll see you again!'

You'll meet without fail on the Midnight Mail

# The Cat of the Railway Train.